The Santa Trap

For my father

for helping me hone my trapping skills

and with apologies to the rest of my family for disturbing their sleep – J.E.

For my parents . . .

and for Santa Claus! – P.B.

Ω

Published by
PEACHTREE PUBLISHERS
1700 Chattahoochee Avenue
Atlanta, Georgia 30318-2112
www.peachtree-online.com

Text copyright © Jonathan Emmett 2009
Illustrations copyright © Poly Bernatene 2009

Originally published in Great Britain in 2009 by Macmillan Children's Books
First United States edition published in 2012 by Peachtree Publishers

Artwork created in digital mixed media

10 9 8 7 6 5 4 3 2

Library of Congress Cataloging-in-Publication Data
Emmett, Jonathan.
The Santa trap / written by Jonathan Emmett ; illustrated by Poly Bernatene.
p. cm.
Summary: Bradley Bartleby has been very bad since the day he was born and finally gets what he deserves after turning
his family's home into a fearsome trap for Santa, who has always given him nothing but socks.
ISBN 978-1-56145-670-3 / 1-56145-670-5
[1. Behavior--Fiction. 2. Santa Claus--Fiction. 3. Christmas--Fiction. 4. Humorous stories.] I. Bernatene, Poly, ill. II. Title.
PZ7.E696San 2012   [E]--dc23
2012004036

Printed in July 2013 in China by WKT

Jonathan Emmett

Poly Bernatene

The Santa Trap

PEACHTREE
ATLANTA

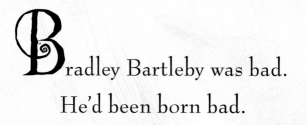

Bradley Bartleby was bad.
He'd been born bad.

Before baby Bradley even left the hospital…

he'd bitten the
midwife on the bottom,

stolen the
doctor's stethoscope,

and emptied his
diaper into his
grandmother's handbag.

And the older Bradley got…

…the badder he became.

Bradley's parents were immensely rich.
They had a huge house with a garden that was big
enough to lose an elephant in.

They knew that the garden was big enough to lose an elephant
in because they'd done exactly that. Bradley had demanded the
elephant as a house pet, but treated it so badly that it escaped
into the garden and was never seen again.

Bradley's parents always gave him whatever he demanded,
not because they thought he deserved it, but because
they were terrified of him.

Every Christmas Mr. Bartleby hired a team of secretaries to type up the huge list of presents that his greedy son demanded from Santa Claus.

Of course Santa knew what a beastly brat Bradley was,
so he never looked at the list. But that didn't mean
that he forgot about Bradley completely.

Santa is such a kindhearted
old fellow that he believes
no child, even one as
bad as Bradley,
should go without a
Christmas present.

So every Christmas morning Bradley would discover that Santa
had left him the same small gift...

"Socks!" howled Bradley.
"Another pair of stupid socks!"

"Never mind, Bradley dear!" cried Mr. and Mrs.
Bartleby as they rushed in with a trolley-load of
presents. "Look, Mummy and Daddy have got
you everything you wanted."

"But I don't want presents from you!"
roared Bradley. "I want presents from
Santa Claus, like everyone else!"
And he stormed back to his room.

The next morning Mr. and Mrs. Bartleby were alarmed to discover that their son had climbed up inside the living-room chimney.

They were even more alarmed to discover that Bradley had nailed several sticks of dynamite around the chimney walls.

"What are you doing, dear?" asked Mrs. Bartleby nervously.

"What does it look like?" scowled Bradley. "I'm building a **trap!**"

"A trap," said Mr. Bartleby. "A trap for what?"

"For Santa Claus," snarled Bradley. "I'm going to catch the fat fool and take every present he's got."

Mr. and Mrs. Bartleby were speechless. In a lifetime of badness this was quite the baddest thing that Bradley had ever tried to do.

Mr. Bartleby was the first to come to his senses.
"Isn't it a little early to be setting a trap?" he gasped.
"It will be a whole year before Santa comes again."

"Oh, this is only the beginning," scoffed Bradley.
"It'll take a whole year to finish it all."

And he was right.

Bradley spent the rest of the winter fixing dynamite inside all the other chimneys…

…and the spring training tigers, which he stole from the local zoo.

He spent the summer fitting guillotines over all the doors and windows...

...and the autumn cutting trapdoors into all the floors.

By the time December came around again, Bradley had turned the entire house into one stupendous...

...Santa
Trap!

By Christmas Eve their home was so dangerous that
Mr. and Mrs. Bartleby had moved out into a hotel,
leaving Bradley alone in the house.

"One last thing!" said Bradley, as he hung his stocking beside the fireplace. He was certain that Santa wouldn't make it that far. But just to make sure, he tied an invisible tripwire to the stocking. The moment anyone touched it, a large metal cage would drop down from above.

"No more **stupid socks!**" thought Bradley.
"This Christmas, I'll get exactly what I want.
This Christmas, I'll get **the whole lot!**"

But as the evening grew darker, Bradley's eyelids grew heavier.
His evil efforts had left him quite exhausted and
he soon fell fast asleep.

It was almost midnight when Bradley was awakened by the roar of
an angry tiger (whose tail had just been stepped on by an elephant).
The house had grown chilly. And when he looked outside, Bradley was
surprised to find the garden covered in a thick blanket of snow.

Shivering with cold, Bradley decided to light a fire.

It was only when the flames began to lick up the chimney

that Bradley remembered the dynamite…

"YEEEAAOOOW!"

The explosion blew Bradley right through the
living-room window and out into the rosebushes below.

Cursing loudly, Bradley struggled free
of the thorny stems. He had barely
caught his breath when six sleek,
stripy shapes came bounding
toward him out of the snow.

"Nice kitties," squealed Bradley as he fled back through the rosebushes with the tigers snapping at his heels.

The tigers chased Bradley around the garden twice before he was able to lose them (by diving into a heap of fresh elephant dung) and creep back to the house.

Determined not to be caught in any more of his own traps, Bradley took a deep breath and prepared himself before opening the front door.

"Aha!" he cried triumphantly as he leaped clear of the falling guillotine.

"Ahaaargh!" he cried miserably as he fell through the trapdoor.

Some time later, as the sun rose on Christmas morning, a scratched, scraped, and badly bruised Bradley limped back to the living room.

There wasn't much of the fireplace left but, amazingly, his stocking was still hanging up. And, even more amazingly, Bradley could see that there was something inside!

Bradley hobbled over, tore
down the stocking, and…

CLANG!

The metal cage dropped right over him.

Bradley let out a long sigh.
He knew that he was beaten.
So he slumped down inside
the cage and emptied his
stocking onto the floor.

For the first time ever, Santa had left
Bradley more than one present.
There was a big box of bandages,
a large jar of antiseptic, and...

… a nice new pair of socks!